Monsters One to Ten

By Emily Thompson
Illustrated by Tom Leigh

LEVEL **Pre 1** READER

READING LEVEL

Published by Dalmatian Press, LLC. All rights reserved.
Printed in Luogang, Guangdong, China.

The DALMATIAN PRESS name is a trademark of Dalmatian Publishing Group,
Franklin, Tennessee 37068-2068. 1-866-418-2572. DalmatianPress.com
No part of this book may be reproduced or copied in any form without written permission
from the copyright owner. CE15074/0113

One tire...

...makes a fun swing.

Two hands…

...make a yummy lunch.

Three snowballs...

...make a cold snowman.

Four letters...

...make Elmo's name.

Five music makers...

...make a jazzy band.

Six friends make a tall tower.

Seven stars make
the Big Dipper.

Eight patches...

...make a comfy quilt.

Nine players make
a baseball team.

Ten monsters…

...make a big mess!